N ederlands
l etterenfonds
dutch foundation
for literature

This book was published with the support
of the Dutch Foundation for Literature
and the Mondriaan Fund.

First published in the UK in 2017 by Lemniscaat Ltd,
Kemp House, 152 City Road, London EC1V 2NX
Distributed worldwide by Thames & Hudson,
181A High Holborn, London WC1V 7QX

ISBN 13: 978-1-78807-010-2 (Hardcover)
Printing and binding: Wilco, Amersfoort
First UK edition

www.lemniscaat.co.uk

FSC
www.fsc.org

MIX
Papier van
verantwoorde herkomst
FSC® C004472

Alice Hoogstad

MONSTER BOOK

LEMNISCAAT

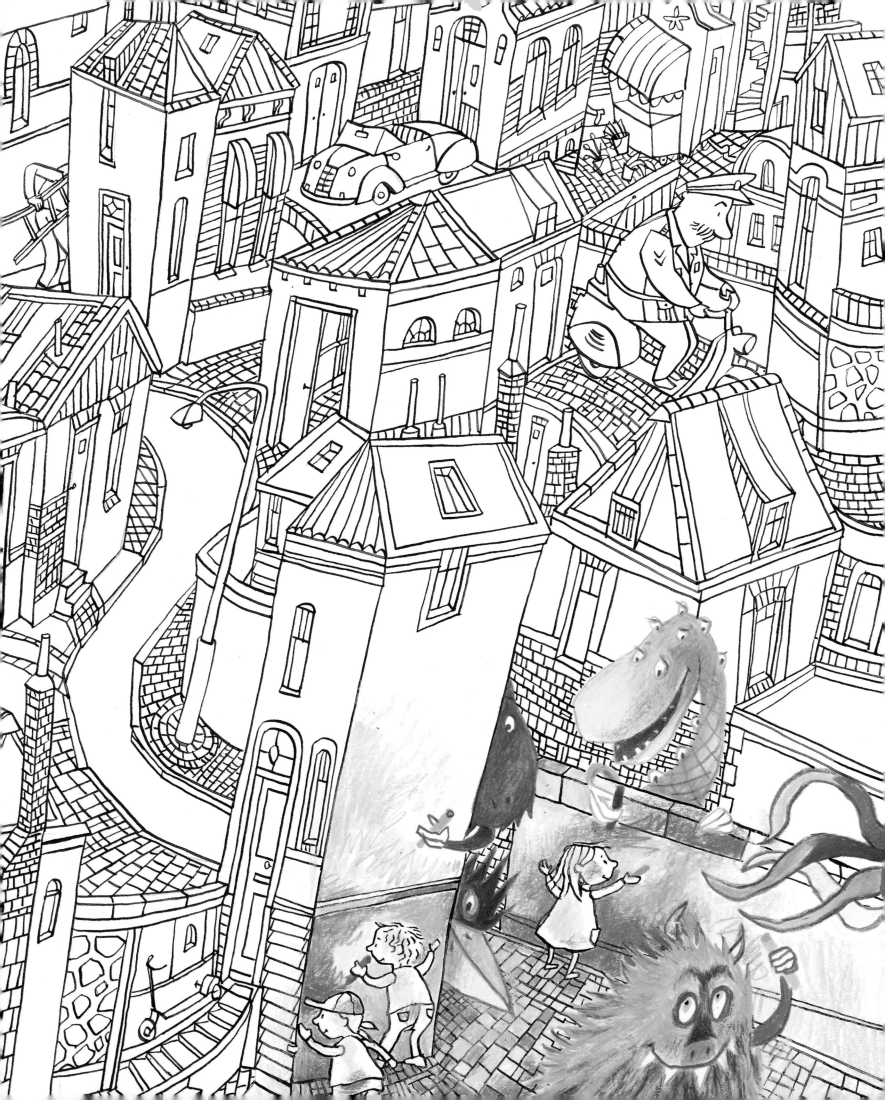